GEMSTONES OF THE WORLD

DIVING FOR PEARLS

Published in 2018 by The Rosen Publishing Group, Inc.
29 East 21st Street, New York, NY 10010

First Edition

Editor: Theresa Morlock
Book Design: Reann Nye

Photo Credits: Cover Laurent Renault/Shutterstock.com; p. 4 ArtCookStudio/Shutterstock.com; p. 5 Everett - Art/Shutterstock.com; p. 6 Niranjan Gaikwad/Shutterstock.com; p. 7 TunedIn by Westend61/Shutterstock.com; p. 8 Maciej Toporowicz, NYC/Moment/Getty Images; p. 9 nikitabuida/Shutterstock.com; p. 10 YANGYANG FANG/Shutterstock.com; p. 11 humphery/Shutterstock.com; p. 12 Valentyn Volkov/Shutterstock.com; p. 13 Andy Bardon/National Geographic Magazines/Getty Images; p. 14 Toscanini/Shutterstock.com; p. 15 Popperfoto/Getty Images; p. 16 Artelier/Shutterstock.com; p. 17 Josh Humbert/National Geographic/Getty Images; p. 18 papa studio/Shutterstock.com; p. 19 Doug Rosa/Corbis/Getty Images; p. 20 Denis Rozhnovsky/Shutterstock.com; p. 21 Dinodia Photo/Passage/Getty Images; p. 22 Lyubov Tolstova/Shutterstock.com.

Cataloging-in-Publication Data

Names: Morlock, Rachael.
Title: Diving for pearls / Rachael Morlock.
Description: New York : PowerKids Press, 2018. | Series: Gemstones of the world | Includes index.
Identifiers: ISBN 9781538328279 (pbk.) | ISBN 9781508164227 (library bound) | ISBN 9781538328330 (6 pack)
Subjects: LCSH: Pearls--Juvenile literature. | Cultured pearls--Juvenile literature.
Classification: LCC TS755.P3 M667 2018 | DDC 639.412--dc23

Manufactured in the United States of America

CPSIA Compliance Information: Batch Batch #BW18PK: For Further Information contact Rosen Publishing, New York, New York at 1-800-237-9932

CONTENTS

A TIMELESS TREASURE

Pearls may be found in lakes, rivers, and oceans around the world. Each one has its own special shape, size, and color. Pearls have never gone out of style! Over 4,000 years ago, people in Mesopotamia used them for **jewelry** and decoration. Pearls have been a **symbol** of **elegance** for many years.

Throughout history, explorers have traveled great distances and divers have entered dangerous waters searching for this prize. Today, more people than ever before value the natural beauty of pearls.

During the 1500s, when this portrait was painted, pearls were only available to royalty and the very rich. This woman's fashionable pearl earrings and necklace show that she was wealthy.

HOW ARE THEY MADE?

Pearls are different from Earth's other gemstones because they're made inside living creatures! Pearls are created by mollusks such as oysters and mussels. Mollusks have a soft body and no backbone. They usually live in a shell.

Pearls form when an outside object works its way into the mollusk's soft inner body. The mollusk's body reacts by releasing a hard **substance** called nacre to protect itself. The nacre covers the object, forming layer after layer around it until it becomes a smooth pearl.

HIDDEN GEMS

Ancient people created stories to explain pearls. The Romans thought they were oysters' tears, while people in India believed they were dewdrops caught by clams. The Greeks said pearls formed when the sea was struck by lightning.

Pearls that form naturally are very rare, or uncommon. They can be found in less than 1 in 10,000 wild oysters! No two pearls are exactly the same.

WHAT IS A CULTURED PEARL?

Natural pearls are rare and difficult to find. A way to **mimic** natural pearl formation was developed in the early 1900s. An outside object is carefully **implanted** in a mollusk. The mollusk is returned to the water and begins to coat the object with nacre.

After several months or even a few years, the pearl is ready to be **harvested**. Pearls formed this way are called cultured pearls. This type of pearl farming is called perliculture.

HIDDEN GEMS

Many people think pearls are started from a single grain of sand. In fact, pearls usually start from organic substances, or substances from a living thing. Most natural pearls form when a **parasite** tunnels into a mollusk.

At a cultured pearl farm in Vietnam, a worker places an **irritant** into an oyster. The irritant is usually a small piece of tissue or shell from another mollusk.

FRESHWATER PEARLS

Pearls that are formed in mollusks in rivers, lakes, and streams are called freshwater pearls. Many of the pearls from Europe, North America, and China come from freshwater sources. The mussels that create these pearls live in shallow waters. They produce 95 percent of the pearls sold today.

Freshwater pearl mussels can make several pearls at a time. Sometimes they can make as many as 30 to 50! The pearls are shiny and come in many colors, including white, pink, and purple.

HIDDEN GEMS

The nacre with which a mollusk creates pearls also forms its shell. This shell substance is called mother-of-pearl. People have used mother-of-pearl throughout history to make shiny buttons, decorations, and art.

Pearl mussels are attached to nets and placed in the water until the pearls are ready for harvesting. In this picture, a man checks mussels at a lake in Jiujiang, China.

MARINE PEARLS

Pearls that form in ocean mollusks are known as marine pearls. Most come from oysters that live in salt water, but they are also found in clams. From ancient times until the beginning of perliculture in the early 1900s, divers usually gathered pearls from parts of the Indian Ocean.

Today, marine pearls are also harvested near Australia, the Polynesian islands, Japan, and other coastal areas. Marine pearls can be white, cream, silver, golden, black, or gray with shades of green, blue, and purple.

HIDDEN GEMS

The largest known natural pearl was found in the Philippines. This pearl formed in a giant clam. It weighs 75 pounds (34 kg) and measures 1 foot (0.3 m) wide and 2.2 feet (0.7 m) long.

These black pearls were grown on a pearl farm in Polynesia.

COLLECTING PEARLS

Collecting pearls can be a dangerous business. To gather marine pearls, divers must swim at least 10 feet below the surface. They face the risk of decompression illness, which makes divers sick if they surface too quickly after a deep dive.

Divers are also put in danger by sea creatures. In Australia, for example, divers risk attacks from sharks, poisonous fish, sea snakes, crocodiles, and jellyfish. Harvesting freshwater pearls is easier since the waters are not as deep and there are fewer predators.

HIDDEN GEMS

For many divers in the past, the shell and meat of a mollusk were more valuable than any pearl it might contain. At one time in Polynesia, pearls were so unimportant that children may have played with them like marbles!

This picture was taken in Japan in 1959. It shows a female diver collecting oysters for pearls.

PEARLS IN THE WORLD

Only healthy mollusks can make pearls. If there are problems in a mollusk's **habitat**, it can affect not only its ability to create pearls but also to survive.

Pollution has caused many pearl mussels to suffer. Within the past 50 years in North America, 35 **species** have become extinct, meaning they've died out completely. There are more than 60 species at risk of extinction. Collecting pearls can also hurt mollusk populations. In several places, harvesting too many pearls has changed the **ecosystem**.

Black-lipped pearl oysters, like the ones pictured here, have been harmed by overfishing. Pearl farming has helped reestablish their populations.

PRECIOUS PEARLS

Unlike other gemstones, pearls don't need many finishing touches. After being removed from the mollusk, they are washed and **polished**. Then they're ready to use!

The qualities that make a pearl valuable are its size, color, shape, smoothness, and luster, or the pearl's ability to shine and **reflect** light. The way a pearl looks and feels depends on the kind of mollusk that made it, the mollusk's nacre, where in the mollusk it was created, and how long it took to form.

HIDDEN GEMS

People discovered ways to create artificial, or fake, pearls thousands of years ago. Fake pearls are smoother and lack the deep luster of real pearls. Today, they're often made with glass beads, fish scales, and other things.

The most popular pearls are smooth and round, but pearls can also be pear shaped, oval, or baroque, meaning uneven in shape. Larger pearls are more valuable.

PEARL POWER

Since ancient times, people have used pearls to show their power, wealth, and good taste. Pearls were sewn into fine clothing or worn as jewelry by royalty. Churches and other places displayed pearls in religious objects.

However, pearls can also be used in unexpected ways. People practicing traditional Chinese or Indian medicine grind pearls into powders that are eaten or made into creams. The ground pearls are believed to treat skin problems, slow the effects of aging, and make people live longer.

Bābur, a 16th-century Muslim leader, is shown draped in pearls as a sign of his importance. The round shape of a pearl symbolizes perfection and completeness in Muslim society.

PEARLS OF WISDOM

Mollusks have lived on Earth and made pearls for about 530 million years! Since humans discovered the joy of pearls, these gemstones have been valued and sought after. More pearls are produced now than ever before because of pearl farming. This makes them more affordable.

Today, pearls represent elegance and purity. They are as popular as ever and a great deal easier to acquire. Pearls are a reminder that great beauty can often be found in unexpected places.

GLOSSARY

ecosystem: A natural community of living and nonliving things.

elegance: Grace and style.

habitat: The natural home for plants, animals, and other living things.

harvest: To gather or collect a crop.

implant: To insert in a living body.

irritant: An object that causes discomfort.

jewelry: Objects worn for decoration that are made of special materials.

mimic: To copy the way something looks, acts, or sounds.

parasite: A living thing that lives in, on, or with another living thing and often harms it.

polish: To rub something to make it smooth and shiny.

reflect: To throw back light, heat, or sound.

species: A group of plants or animals that are all the same kind.

substance: A kind of material, or something from which something else can be made.

symbol: Something that stands for something else.

INDEX

WEBSITES

Due to the changing nature of Internet links, PowerKids Press has developed an online list of websites related to the subject of this book. This site is updated regularly. Please use this link to access the list: www.powerkidslinks.com/gotw/pearl